PIRATE GOLD

MARCIE AND AMANDA MYSTERIES

Glen Ebisch

Published by As You Like It Press, 2021.

This is a work of fiction. Similarities to real people, places, or events are entirely coincidental.

PIRATE GOLD

First edition. September 18, 2021.

Written by Glen Ebisch.

Table of Contents

Chapter One

$\mathbf{M}$arcie Ducasse peered out through the windshield as the rain
beat down on the hood like a drummer warming to his solo.
Visibility had only gotten worse since she had left the office of
Roaming New England Magazine along Route 1 in Wells, Maine.
She heartily wished that she hadn't stayed the extra hour to
proofread the last article for the next edition. Amanda had suggested
that Marcie leave earlier, since it had been threatening to storm all
day, but Marcie was determined to finish the story about
extraterrestrials in Vermont. It was the final piece in her *Weird
Happenings* column for the fall issue coming out in October. Since it
was already early September, they had to get the proofs to the printer
by Wednesday.

Marcie suddenly found herself wanting to get out of the rain, and
although her condo was only a couple of miles away, nothing
awaited her there aside from her own company, the television, and
some leftover Chinese food. She decided to stop. The rain kicked up
a notch, just as she spotted The Tern Inn on her left. She'd eaten
there several times before on nights when she craved the presence of
people. She didn't go there for company—just being able to see
folks and pick up random snatches of conversation was enough. It
provided a pleasant background to eat good food. Feeling her tires
lose their grip slightly on the wet road as she made a sharp turn into
the inn's parking lot, Marcie pulled into a space as close as she could
get to the front door and dashed inside.

The lobby was warm and welcoming. A young woman stood
behind the wooden counter that ran along the right side of the lobby.
She said hello to Marcie, glancing at her hopefully, probably because
not many guests stayed overnight at the inn during the week once the
summer season was over. Marcie smiled and indicated that she was
going into the bar on her left. The young woman nodded with sad
resignation.

Marcie walked into the taproom, which was heavy on mahogany
and atmosphere. The bartender, a fit looking guy in his forties, said
hello as if he remembered her. Marcie doubted she was that
memorable, but then there weren't very many women who dined

alone at the Inn so it was possible. In fact, aside from two or three couples, she didn't remember seeing people eating in the bar even in season. There was a formal dining room across the hall, and she figured most of the guests ate there. Six older men were seated at one end of the bar. They glanced at her incuriously as she walked in and took a seat. They quickly went back to their conversation. Body language and the desultory chatter indicated that they were regulars.

"Nice to see you again," the bartender said with a pleasantly professional smile as he handed her a menu. "It's a wild night out there."

"But nice in here," she said, looking toward the end of the room where a cheerful fire was blazing.

"Yeah, it's a bit early in the season, but the fire helps take the chill off." He glanced toward the guys at the bar. "And the company is what it is. Can I get you something to drink while you look over the menu?"

Marcie ordered a white wine and settled down to study the choices. She rubbed her hands over her face and pressed them on her temples, trying to relax her eyes after a long day squinting at the computer screen. When the bartender came back with her wine, she ordered the codfish cakes and a small salad. She liked that he just nodded and didn't bother to flatter her by saying what a good choice she had made, as if this had been her greatest challenge of the day. Marcie put her phone to one side on the table and sipped her wine, determined to ignore e-mails and all the other nagging urgencies of her job. She looked across the room at the fire and allowed the deep-voiced conversation of the guys at the bar to lull her into a state of relaxation. The contrast between the rain beating a tattoo on the window next to her and the warm fustiness of the room only made her feel more comfortable and protected. When her salad arrived, she began to eat with enthusiasm, suddenly realizing how long it had been since her lunch of yogurt and a piece of fruit. She was so focused on her food that it took her a moment to realize that someone was standing on the other side of her table.

"Do you mind if I join you?" said a voice with a slight nasal twang.

Marcie looked up. The man standing there was probably in his late thirties with dark, curly hair that looked like it hadn't seen a comb in a while. He was of medium height but seemed taller

5

because he was painfully thin. The silver buckle on his wide black belt was cinched in until it looked like it was touching his backbone. He bounced nervously from foot to foot as if he was either on something or had an appointment down the road to get to within the next minute.

"Yes, I mind," Marcie said in a firm voice.

"This isn't what it looks like," he said.

"It looks like some guy bothering me in the middle of my meal," Marcie replied, turning back to her salad.

"I've got a business proposition for you."

"What are you selling: insurance, real estate, or an extended warrantee on my car?"

"Something way better than that. It's something you can use in your column."

Marcie went cold. This wasn't some random nuisance. This was someone who knew who she was. Maybe even someone who had followed her from work. A stalker!

"Really, I can explain everything," he said quickly, spotting the concern on her face. "I'm not here to cause any trouble, but I've got a great story for you." He pulled out a chair and sat down across from her. He leaned forward as if getting ready to whisper.

"Is there a problem here?"

The bartender had materialized next to the table and was sizing up the guy across from Marcie, as if welcoming the opportunity to throw him out into the rain. Marcie seriously thought about it. Although she wanted nothing more than a quiet dinner, the professional side of her was ringing a warning bell that you should never pass up the chance for a good story.

"No problem yet. But if I wave my hand, toss him out."

The bartender nodded and returned to the other side of the room.

"Thanks," the man said, giving her a surprisingly charming smile.

"Don't get too comfortable. What's your name?"

"Marty."

"Marty what?"

He shook his head. "I have to know that you're interested in my story first."

"Did you follow me from work?"

His eyes darted away from hers and he nervously licked his lips. "Yeah, I did. I had to get you alone to tell you my story."

"You could have called me at my office. That would have been private enough."

"I had to meet you face to face to know if I can trust you."

"So what do you think?" Marcie asked, half curious.

"You'll do."

"Yeah. I get that a lot from guys. So what story are you trying to sell me?"

He reached in the pocket of the light jacket he was wearing and took out something small. He placed it on the table; half covering it with his hand while his eyes danced around the room to see if anyone was watching. When he finally removed his hand, Marcie would see that it was an old coin of some sort. She reached forward to touch it, but he swept it off the table in a lightning motion, like a cheap conjuring trick, and returned it to his pocket.

"Okay, I give up. What was it?" Marcie asked.

"A Spanish doubloon, a piece of eight . . . pirate treasure."

"For all I saw, it could have been something you made in your basement."

He frowned. "I've got a map."

Marcie sighed. "Do you know how many people come to me in a year claiming to have a map that will lead to a pirate treasure in New England?"

Marty shook his head.

"A lot."

"But this is a map to Captain Kidd's treasure."

Marcie rolled her eyes. "Worse yet."

"But I have the coin because I've already found the treasure."

Marcie had to admit to herself that this was a new wrinkle. "If you found the treasure, what do you need with me? Take the gold and have a good life."

"I don't just want to be rich."

Another new angle, she thought. "What do you want to be?"

"Famous," he whispered, blushing from his scrawny neck up to the roots of his curly hair.

Marcie smiled, feeling her first sense of connection to the guy. "Well, I can relate to that. So what did you have in mind to make yourself famous?"

"I thought you could go with me and do a story with lots of photographs of me finding the treasure."

"For the second time."

"Would we have to tell people that?"

Marcie nodded. "I'm not going to lie. But I don't see that as a problem, folks aren't going to care if it's your second trip. We could call it a reenactment. They just want to see the gold and hear your story. I'm sure there's a story about how you got the map, too. Right?"

Marty looked across the room, as if trying to decide whether to share. The bartender brought Marcie her fishcakes and gave her a quizzical glance. She nodded to show that things were all right. He asked her if she wanted another glass of wine, and she shook her head. She wanted her wits about her while dealing with treasure guy. When the bartender left, she started to eat, giving Marty time to think.

"His name was Ralph Winston. He owned the house I was boarding in up in Bangor. He was an old guy in his seventies and didn't get around very well. I used to do his shopping for him, buy him some booze, and listen to his stories. He had a son somewhere, but the kid never came around. Winston was kind of bitter about that."

"This Winston is the one who had the map?"

Marty nodded. "He got it from some guy he used to work with, who won it in a poker game."

"You'd think someone along the way would already have found the treasure."

Marty grinned. "I'm sure a lot have tried, but I had an edge."

The cod cake was good and Marcie savored it. "And what was that?" she finally asked.

"I used to be in IT. I know my way around a computer and satellite maps. I used an aerial view to figure out the map." He reached in his pocket and took out a sheet of paper and unfolded it on the table. It looked like it had been folded and unfolded many times. It showed what looked to be an island with various features marked and a lot of writing around the edges. "I put my notes right on the map."

"This is a sheet of paper, but it doesn't look very original. I doubt Captain Kidd used bond paper."

"I'm sure it's been copied over many times since Captain Kidd drew the original. But the point is I found the treasure."

"And you took one coin and left the rest of the treasure there."

"Just for proof that I'd found it."

Marcie took a sip of her wine. "What do you figure the treasure is worth?"

"Hard to say. If you go by the value of the gold alone, a single coin is worth about four hundred, but at auction old coins can go for millions. That's another reason why I want this to go public. I can get the best price if I put it on the open market."

Marcie tapped the map with her index finger. "So what island is this?"

He folded up the map and put it in his pocket. "I got to know that you're in on this before I tell you that."

Marcie frowned. "What would you need from *Roaming New England*?"

"First of all the promise that you would keep all of this confidential until we have the treasure and the story is ready to come out."

"I can promise that."

"The other thing is, I'm a little short of funds, and you'd have to front the money for the expedition."

"How much are we talking about?"

"Only around a thousand."

Marcie thought for a moment. Amanda was very frugal with the budget because Sam Peabody, the owner of the magazine, kept a wary eye on overhead. He often said that most stories were worth less than a hundred dollars. A thousand would be way more than Amanda would be willing to spend, but Marcie had done little other than work and save for the last few years since joining the magazine. A story like this would be a big boost to her reputation, and she could easily afford to cover the costs. It was a simple decision to make.

"We can take care of that, but you have to tell me the location of the island before I go to my boss."

Now it was Marty's turn to pause. Finally he said, "Have you ever heard of Jewell Island?"

"Isn't it somewhere in Casco Bay off of Portland?"

9

"Right. It's the island furthest out, but that's still only about eight miles from Portland."

"So we'd need to get a boat to ferry us out there?"

"Yeah, a private charter would be best. Fewer questions asked. This time of the year there wouldn't be any tourists on the island, especially during the week."

"Would we need transportation once we were out there?"

Marty shook his head. "The whole island is only about a mile long. You can walk anywhere you need to go."

"But the treasure itself must be heavy, we'd have to transport it."

"We'll bring some sacks and divide it up. If we have three or four people we could each carry ten or fifteen pounds. That should do it."

Marcie turned the plan over in her mind. "Sounds easy." Too easy, she thought to herself.

The man paused and a troubled expression came over his face.

"What's wrong?" Marcie asked.

"Well, there is one thing. The legend is that Captain Kidd put a curse on the treasure, and anyone that takes it will die."

"Every self-respecting pirates' treasure has a curse."

"You don't seem very impressed."

"I investigate the supernatural all the time. Ninety-nine percent of the time it's nothing but rumor and hearsay. If something weird does happen, it's usually someone playing a prank or committing a crime."

"What about the other one percent?" Marty asked with a haunted look in his eyes.

"Ah, well that's what makes my job interesting. Sometimes there is an element of the unexplained, where you just have to throw up your hands and say maybe there's more to all this supernatural stuff than I thought. But you've already taken some of the treasure and nothing's happened to you."

"So far." Marty turned and surveyed the quiet, cozy scene around them. "It's just that I've had a funny feeling lately that I'm being watched."

"Probably you've just got the curse on your mind. You're spooked and jumping at shadows. It happens all the time when people get involved with the apparently supernatural. Just keep telling yourself that this is your chance at fame."

The man smiled. "Do you really think I'll be famous?"

Marcie returned his smile. "I'll do my best. Maybe some national publications or even television will pick it up."

"Cool."

"This treasure is on public land, right? We won't be trespassing."

"We'll be free and clear."

Marcie reached into her wallet and handed him a card. "Call me tomorrow afternoon, and I'll give you an update."

Marty stretched a long, thin hand across the table, and Marcie shook it. "To our mutual success," she said.

The man smiled. He stood up and bounced his way out of the room.

Marcie sat at the table, her meal only half finished. She motioned to the bartender and asked for a box to package up what was left. She'd lost her appetite; her mind was filled with the mixture of fear and excitement that came when she was on the trail of a good story.

Chapter Two

Marcie walked up the stairs to her office. *Roaming New England Magazine* rented the second floor of an old house on the beach side of Route 1 in Wells, Maine. A chocolate shop and a cheese store occupied the first floor, and in the nice weather when the windows were open, Marcie found the aromas very tempting. Although she kept fit, no one would ever mistake her body for that of a marathoner. Today her mind was focused on business, however, in particular the need to convince Amanda to allow her to write a story about pirate gold. When Marcie reached the top of the stairs she turned right and walked down the hall to her office. The magazine's quarters were limited. Marcie's office was at one end of the hall, and on the other end was Amanda's slightly larger one. In between was a conference room that they also used as a lounge. Next to it was a small bathroom.

Marcie hung up her coat on the old wooden coat rack that had been there when she had taken over the job several years ago. She sometimes wondered how many of her predecessors had hung coats there and what these people had gone on to do. She turned and glanced out the window. In the distance she could see the ocean, and she imagined a sailing ship flying the Jolly Roger making its way up the coast, heading for Jewell Island. She had written some exciting stories for the *Weird Happenings* column. However, this would certainly be one of the best. But, she reminded herself, she still had to get permission from the boss. As if on cue, she heard footsteps on the stairs and knew that Amanda had arrived. Marcie gave her a few minutes to settle in behind her desk, and then, pasting a happy smile on her face, she headed down the hall.

Amanda was focused on her computer and didn't see Marcie standing in the doorway. As usual Amanda appeared to be dressed in the height of fashion, although Marcie knew she was a smart shopper and didn't spend a lot on her clothes. Being tall and willowy like a fashion model didn't hurt either. Marcie, being a couple of inches shorter and more statuesque, often envied Amanda her natural grace and style. The hours Marcie spent at the gym, however, made her stronger and fitter, which was sometimes a handy attribute in her paranormal investigations.

Marcie cleared her throat and Amanda turned to look at her. She smiled.

"Good morning. Sorry, I didn't see you standing there. I'm so obsessed with getting these last minute edits done that I can hardly think of anything else."

"I had something to discuss with you, but I can come back later," Marcie said.

Amanda gave her a long look, then gestured to the chair in front of her desk. "I can see by the expression on your face that something is going on. Is it something I'm going to be happy to hear about?"

Marcie shrugged and settled into the chair. "I suppose that depends. It is something exciting."

"Oh, God, I never like conversations that begin that way. They always end up with someone in a lot of trouble, usually you and by extension me."

Marcie grinned, "But we're still here, so it hasn't been that bad."

Amanda sighed. "Tell me about it."

Marcie proceeded to recount her conversation with Marty from the night before. Amanda listened carefully, her face remaining expressionless. When Marcie was done, she stared at Amanda, waiting for her response.

"I see two problems with this plan," Amanda said slowly. "The first, and less important one, is that a thousand dollars is our entire travel budget for the next three months. What do we do if another exciting idea comes along next month, as I'm sure it will?"

Marcie opened her mouth to offer to pay for the trip to Jewell Island, but Amanda held up her hand. "That's the less important problem. I can find a way to wangle the money. The major problem is that I can't in good conscience let you go wandering alone on a deserted island with a strange man about whom you know next to nothing. Sam would kill me if I let anything happen to you. He thinks of you as a daughter—a rather wayward daughter, to be sure—but a daughter nonetheless."

Marcie smiled. Although Amanda preferred to blame the magazine's owner, she knew that Amanda herself was the truly protective one and would be the one most upset if anything should happen to her.

13

"Actually, I agree with you on the second problem. And, anyway, we would need a team to carry out this project. Just Marty and I wouldn't be enough muscle. We'd need at least one other person to take photographs and help us carry out the gold. Two would be even better."

"If there is any gold. Too bad we don't have Simon on board anymore. We could really use him."

Simon was a retired college professor who had accompanied Marcie on one of her recent stories, but he had married a wealthy woman named Sheila Little, whom he had met on that adventure, moved to Connecticut, and stopped working for the magazine. The last Marcie had spoken with him he was reveling in the life of a kept husband.

"Maybe you could come along," Marcie suggested. Amanda wasn't much for fieldwork, but she had certainly done it in the past when necessary.

Amanda considered the idea. "A little time out on Casco Bay might be fun, but I still think we need another man along for protection."

Marcie was between boyfriends or she might have had someone to suggest. Although she thought that she could handle just about anything herself, she appreciated Amanda's point that Marty was an unknown quantity, and having another man along might be prudent.

"What about your fiancé Richard?"

Amanda frowned. "You know he hardly ever leaves the hotel, and he's not exactly an outdoorsman."

Marcie almost said at least he was better than nothing, but decided that wouldn't be very complimentary. Richard was the manager of a local resort hotel. He was focused completely on making that enterprise a success, to the point of even living on the premises. Amanda frequently complained that his conversation revolved almost exclusively around the latest news in the hospitality industry. He had managed to change focus a few months back, long enough to ask Amanda to marry him. She had reluctantly agreed, and then changed her mind. They now seemed to have a kind of on again off again engagement that Marcie had trouble following.

"He is a big guy," Marcie pointed out.

"But he's rather nonphysical," Amanda said, leading Marcie to wonder if there was a more general problem in their relationship.

14

"Image is everything. Just looking at him should make Marty hesitant to start trouble."

"You have a point. I'll ask him, but I may not be able to convince him to take a day off from the hotel, especially to go wandering around some island."

"Maybe the lure of pirate treasure will attract him," said Marcie.

"Only if he can think of a way it might increase bookings at the hotel."

"Maybe we can convince Marty to let him put the treasure on display in the lobby for a weekend."

Amanda smiled. "That might be enough. Anyway, I'll ask him."

• • • •

MARCIE SPENT THE REST of the morning finishing up some final details on the next issue. She had just eaten lunch at her desk and looked over emails she had received about possible supernatural happenings in New England when she heard the heavy tread of feet coming up the stairs. Since Sam was intent on keeping costs razor thin, they had no receptionist, and it was Marcie's job to look out into the hallway when people arrived and ask their business. When two men appeared in the hall outside her office door, one short and muscular and the other tall and thin, she did just that. The short one cleared his throat as if about to spit and held a badge close to her face.

"Is there a Marcie Ducasse here?" he asked gruffly, staring at her as if he already suspected the answer.

For an instant Marcie considered saying she'd never heard of her because this sounded like trouble, but then she decided that a denial would only get her in deeper.

"I'm Marcie Ducasse," she said in as firm a voice as she could muster.

The man nodded. "I'm Detective Malone and this is Detective Lancaster," he said, nodding to the tall man. The second man also opened a wallet and flashed credentials that she barely saw. Then they came into the office and took seats as if she had asked them to sit down.

"Make yourselves comfortable, gentlemen. How can I help you?" she said trying to sound polite while bordering on frosty.

These public servants were obviously not interested in making a good impression on the public.

"Do you know a Marty Walker?"

"I met a man named Marty yesterday. He didn't tell me his last name."

"Is this your card?" the short cop asked, holding up one of her business cards in a clear plastic bag. The tall one looked around the office as if he was just there to observe.

"Yes, it is."

"Did you give a card like this to Marty when you met him yesterday?"

Marcie nodded.

"Is this the man you gave the card to?"

The tall cop produced a photograph and handed it to his partner, who placed it on the desk in front of Marcie. She stared at the face, which somehow looked like Marty but in a way didn't. His head was back and his eyes half-open. He was very white.

"That looks like him," she said slowly. "But he seems different."

"Most folks do when they're dead." The tall cop finally spoke.

Marcie's breath caught in her chest, and she had to make a conscious effort to exhale.

"What happened to him?"

"Maybe you can tell us," the short cop said. "What did you talk about when you saw him yesterday?"

"Pirate treasure."

Her answer got more of a reaction than she expected. The tall cop actually looked directly at her, and the other one appeared angry. "Maybe you'd better explain what you're talking about," he said in a tight voice, as if he thought she was making fun of him.

Marcie went on to give a pretty complete summary of her conversation with Marty. When she was done, the two cops glanced at each other expressionlessly.

"So you actually saw a treasure map?" the shorter cop asked.

"I saw something that looked like a map of an island. He told me it was a map of Jewell Island, and he said it showed where to find Captain Kidd's treasure."

The tall cop smiled. "And you believed him?"

"Not fully. But he did have the coin."

"Which you barely saw."

16

"True, but he had nothing to gain by lying to me. I was going to look into financing the expedition, but I wasn't giving him any money personally."

"Some people lie just to lie," the short cop said.

Marcie shrugged. "But since he was murdered, there must have been something to his story."

"We didn't say he was murdered," the short cop said, giving her a sharp glance.

"I doubt you'd be here asking me questions if he'd died of a heart attack."

The tall cop smiled. "Okay, he was murdered. Someone stabbed him through the heart."

"Where did this happen?"

"At the Arrow Motel down in York," the tall cop said. "Do you know it?" The short one gave him a look as if he'd said too much.

Marcie shook her head. "And I assume you didn't find a map or the coin."

"Just a nickel and two quarters," the short one said. "And your card."

The sudden thought struck Marcie that they might suspect her of having murdered Marty. After all, she'd admitted knowing about the map and the coin. It would be natural to speculate that she might have decided to steal the map and get the treasure for herself.

"Marty thought someone was following him," Marcie repeated again for emphasis.

"So you say," the short cop said with a smirk. "But as far as we know, you're the only one who knew Marty was running around with this map. What did you do last night after you left the bar?"

"I went back to my condo and spent the night there."

"Can anyone corroborate that?" the short cop asked. "Any husband or boyfriend."

"I was alone all night."

"Convenient," he said, glancing at his partner.

Amanda appeared in the doorway. "All right, gentlemen, I've called the magazine's attorney, and he's informed me that Ms. Ducasse should not answer any more questions unless he's present," she said in he most formal vice. "He'll be here shortly if you'd care to wait."

17

"We could always take her downtown and book her," short cop said with a grin.

"Need I remind you that we are a magazine focused on New England? It's been a while since we've done an exposé, but we could always make an exception and do one on the abuse of police power along the southern coast of Maine. That might actually grow our readership."

Amanda stood in the doorway looking relaxed, tall, and stylish. A cool smile played along her lips.

The tall cop stood up. "I guess we can leave it there for now. If new facts come in, we'll talk to you again."

The shorter cop gave Marcie a long look, which she figured was meant to be intimidating, before he left the office. Neither woman said anything until the two pairs of feet had clomped down the stairs and the door had shut.

"Thanks for coming to the rescue. That was getting awkward. What are we going to tell the attorney when he shows up?"

"Oh, I didn't actually call Fletcher, Goldman and Russell. The first thing they would do is contact Sam, and he'd want to know what we were up to. You know Sam, he's worse than the police."

"You were very convincing."

"No sense lying if you're going to be half-hearted about it."

Marcie frowned. "But I guess our story is over before it gets started. I figure the killer has the map, and is probably half-way to Jewell Island by now."

"Maybe," Amanda said, gazing thoughtfully out the window.

"You don't think so."

"It's possible, of course, but Marty sounded like a nervous kind of guy. It seems to me that he would have hidden the map where it would be hard to find."

"Okay, but wouldn't the killer have threatened him until he told where it was?"

"That's one scenario. Another is that Marty tries to disarm the guy and gets killed without ever revealing the whereabouts of the map."

"So the map is wherever he hid it. Maybe I should take a little drive to the Arrow Motel."

18

Amanda nodded. "I can finish up the remaining changes for the next issue. But be prudent. If someone calls the police on you, we will be needing legal help."

"I'll be the soul of discretion."

Chapter Three

The Arrow Motel was on a side street off Route One on the northern edge of York. Unlike most of the motels and resorts along the main road, it looked like it hadn't been updated since it was built fifty years ago. It was composed of a line of rooms with parking in front, and on one end was a doublewide room with a sign in the window that said "office." There was one car in front of a unit and one next to the office. Marcie took an empty spot nearby and walked into the small lobby. A man who looked to be in his eighties, slowly got up from the chair in front of a tiny television and strolled up to the desk.

"Looking for a room?" he asked. There was a hint of surprise in his voice as if she didn't look like his average customer. Perhaps having any customer at all surprised him.

"I'm with *Roaming New England Magazine*," Marcie said with as much authority in her tone as she could muster, hoping he'd think the publication equivalent to the *New York Times*. "I heard that you had a murder here last night."

"I wouldn't know anything about that. I only come on at noon," he replied, already starting to turn back toward his television.

"Are you saying the guy on duty before you wouldn't have bothered to fill you in on a little thing like that?"

He paused and glanced back at her. "The police said that if some folks came around asking, I shouldn't let them know anything."

"Do you always do what the police tell you to do?" Marcie asked with a smile.

The man took a moment as if reviewing his life and then smiled back. "What is it you want, exactly?"

"Not much. A chance to look around the room where it happened would be helpful."

"No pictures, and you don't take anything."

"Okay."

"A hundred fifty bucks." His dry lips formed a firm line as if those were his last words.

"A hundred," Marcie replied.

He licked his lips. "One twenty-five."

Marcie reached in her purse. She had emptied out the rainy day fund before leaving the office, figuring you couldn't very well put a bribe on a credit card. She slowly counted out the bills on the counter, so he could keep up. He carefully inspected each one as if expecting counterfeit. Maybe that happened a lot at the Arrow Motel.

"I'll walk you up there and watch you as you look around."

Marcie shook her head. "You can stand outside the door to make sure I don't take anything, but I look around on my own with the door closed."

The man took a key off a hook on the wall and came around the counter.

"C'mon. It's room ten."

She slowed to his halting pace as they walked past the empty rooms. Marcie wondered if they did a better business in the summer. She figured they must, unless the motel was a front for some other kind of business.

He stopped in front of number ten and opened the door.

"Ten minutes," he said, turning to walk away. "I'll be at the desk counting."

Marcie didn't argue. Given the size of the room, what couldn't be found in ten minutes would only be found by a crew with crowbars to dismantle the place. Keeping her distance, she walked past the man and pulled the door closed behind her. She had been ready to face disgusting odors, but aside from some mustiness, which was probably the natural smell in every room at the motel, it seemed fine. There was a dark stain on the floor where Marty's body had probably been.

She took a quick survey of the room. It consisted of a bedroom with a double bed, a closet, and a bathroom. The walls were decorated with pictures of waves that looked as old as the ocean itself, and there was a single lamp designed like a ship's wheel. Across from the bed was a dresser. Marcie went through the empty drawers, and then pulled them all out to check on the bottoms. The bedside table was equally uninteresting except for a Bible, which she leafed through without luck. She checked the top shelf in the closet and looked inside the toilet tank in the bathroom. Trying not to strain her back she checked under the mattress and under the bed.

The police had probably examined all these places, but they had been looking for the murder weapon, not a map. Finishing up, she checked behind the art on the walls, which revealed only that the walls hadn't been painted in decades, but little else. Another quick survey of the room didn't reveal any loose areas of carpeting where something might have been hidden, and the ceiling wasn't made of acoustic tiles that could be removed.

Marcie walked back to the office. Her friend was in front of the television watching a quiz show.

"Who found the body?" she asked over the noise of the studio audience.

He hesitated as if weighing his chances of getting more money. Marcie gave him a hard stare.

"The maid. She goes around at eleven to make sure everyone has checked out who's only paid for a night. I guess she got a shock. I got called in early because the kid who was on the desk went down to see what had happened and didn't feel well. Kids today don't have any grit."

"What happened to the victim's car?"

"The cops took it. A window had been smashed out."

"How many people stayed here last night?"

"Just the guy who got killed."

"There's another car here now."

"He just came in a couple of hours ago."

Marcie nodded and turned to leave.

"When do you think your story will be coming out?" the clerk suddenly asked.

"Not for a few months. It's a magazine."

"Since it's that far off, maybe you could use a picture of me for the story. By then no one will care who I talked to."

At first she was going to refuse, but then she felt a little sorry for an old guy with a dead end job. Plus he was right; every story needed some photos. She held up her phone and snapped his picture.

"And my name is Bert Fox. You want to write that down. It's spelled just like the animal."

"I'll remember it," Marcie assured him as she left the office.

• • • •

22

wandered into her bedroom where the mattress had been pulled off its foundation; her clothes were tossed across the floor, and her shoes thrown with evident frustration across the room. She was glad that she didn't use more beauty products than she did because they had all been dumped into the sink. She also saw where a back windowpane had been broken, allowing the intruder to get inside.

Stunned, Marcie drifted back to the dining area and collapsed down on the one dining room chair that was not overturned. She took several deep breaths to try to regain her composure and thought about what she was seeing. The first thought was that she had been robbed, but her personal laptop still sat on the table in her dining room and her flat screen television was untouched. Although no expert on theft, it seemed to her that they would be among the most common items to be stolen. A chill suddenly went up Marcie's spine, and she returned to her front door and put on the lock and chain. What if someone had broken into her condo looking for a very specific item, for example a pirate map? That would mean that the person's search of Marty's motel room had been as fruitless as her own. It might also mean that the intruder would soon be back to interrogate her in person as to the whereabouts of the map. Somehow Marcie felt that being unable to answer that question would be unacceptable, and she could easily end up just as dead as Marty.

She could call the police, but the local cops would probably write it off as a common burglary. If she told them about the possible link to Marty's death, they would contact tweedledum and tweedledee, the two detectives from York. They'd figure she must have the map, and arrest her for having murdered Marty.

She rushed into her bedroom and pulled out her suitcase. Not paying much attention to what she was doing, Marcie began picking up items of clothing from the floor and stuffing them into her bag. She did the same with toiletries and some cash she had in reserve. Glancing out the front window to see if the coast was clear, she charged out the front door and ran to her car. Once she had locked the doors, Marcie sat for a moment checking out the neighborhood for signs that she was being watched. She didn't see anyone loitering in the parking lot, but when she left, Marcie took several side streets that had no traffic to make certain she wasn't being followed. Then she headed directly to her destination. She pulled in between two cars in the apartment parking lot, so her vehicle wouldn't stand out.

Grabbing her suitcase, she walked across to the front door, which was under a green canopy. She went into the lobby and rang the buzzer for the apartment she wanted. Marcie identified herself and the inside door was buzzed open. She took the elevator up to the fifth floor, went down the hall, and knocked on the door. The door opened and Amanda stood there, perfectly made up as always, and gave her a puzzled look.

"I think I need help," Marcie said.

Chapter Four

"Wh   hat we need is a plan," said Amanda. She had made them both cups of tea and listened without speaking while Marcie described the scene in her apartment. This was the first time she had spoken.

"I had a plan, but it doesn't seem to be working out."

Amanda smiled. "You know what the fighter Mike Tyson said, 'Everyone has a plan until he gets hit.'"

Marcie gave her a confused look. "Aside from the fact that I'm stunned you even know who Mike Tyson is, what is that supposed to mean?"

"Let me put it another way, plans are made to be revised to fit new circumstances. You didn't expect the killer to know where you live or expect him to think you have the map. Well he does, so now we need a change of plan."

"Okay, what do you have in mind?"

"I think you're right not to involve the police at this stage. Those two detectives seem fixated on blaming you for the murder. Having had your condo tossed would just confirm their suspicions. You also can't return to work. Whoever killed Marty had probably been following him for some time. No doubt he saw Marty follow you from the magazine offices. He's likely to look for you there."

"So where do I go?"

"You stay right here."

Marcie frowned. "I appreciate the offer, but I can't live here forever."

"Hopefully, it won't be that long. No matter how incompetent the police may seem, they are going to seriously investigate a murder, and it's likely they'll get some clues that will lead them away from you and toward the real killer. That means whoever murdered Marty isn't going to want to hang around here any longer than necessary. When he can't find you, he'll likely give up and move on."

Marcie considered what Amanda had planned. "Let's say you're right. That means the killer is watching our offices, so it's not safe for either one of us to return to work. How are we going to put the magazine out?"

"We need our laptops from the office. Once we have those, we can work remotely from here. I'll go into the office and get them. He won't bother me because he doesn't think I have the map, since Marty made contact with you while you were on your own. I'll make sure I'm not followed back from the office, then we'll be all set."

"No way I'm letting you go back to the office by yourself. This killer could be lying in wait for anyone he sees go into our offices. He might figure you can tell him where I am."

Amanda nodded. "Maybe you're right. We go together and get the stuff we need. If we're lucky, he's already off somewhere hiding from the police. Tomorrow morning right before nine, when the mail arrives, we get what we need and get out."

"What about tonight?" asked Marcie. "I hate to impose, but . . . "

"You'll stay in my guest room. It's not safe for you to remain at your condo. The killer might come back looking for the map."

"A map I don't have."

"I wonder where it is," Amanda said slowly. "The killer searched his motel room and Marty's car, but apparently he hasn't found it yet."

"Marty was an odd guy. He probably had a special secret hiding place. The map most likely will never be found."

"Well, we'll worry about that tomorrow. Now it's time to get some sleep."

Amanda took Marcie into the guest room. As Marcie would have expected, it was tastefully decorated, ready and waiting for a guest. Amanda had never spoken about having any overnight guests, but obviously she was prepared for the eventuality.

"Did you bring night clothes?" asked Amanda. "I have extras, but they'll probably be rather long on you."

"I'm pretty sure I threw a sweatshirt and a pair of yoga pants in my suitcase as I was heading out the door. That will be fine."

Amanda's expression remained neutral, but somehow Marcie got the impression that she usually slept in silk. Once she had acquainted Marcie with the hall bathroom that was exclusively for her use and shown her where everything was located, Amanda wished her goodnight. A few minutes later Marcie crawled into the plush bed fully expecting to lie awake worrying about what tomorrow would bring, but within minutes she was sound asleep.

• • • •

NEITHER ONE OF THEM said much over breakfast, which was a simple affair of cold cereal, orange juice, and coffee. Marcie liked a large breakfast and frequently went out to a local diner for eggs and bacon or pancakes. But she knew Amanda was a picky eater, so she was happy with what she got. After breakfast they dressed. Instead of wearing her usual dressy work clothes, which usually involved a skirt or dress, Amanda chose a pair of designer jeans and a loose-fitting silk blouse, which she said would enable her to run more easily if she had to. Marcie didn't say anything, but eyed Amanda's flats, that didn't look like they'd stay on her feet for more then five steps. Marcie herself was wearing scruffy workout shoes, a sweatshirt, and a pair of loose fitting hiking pants. She also had a sturdy utility knife in her pocket because you never knew when it would come in handy.

They left so they would arrive just before the nine o'clock mail delivery. It would only take them five minutes to grab the mail, gather up their computers, and be back out on the road. Amanda took a circuitous route to the office that involved narrow side roads, so they could check to see if they were being followed. Marcie spent most of her time looking out the back window, and didn't spot anyone suspicious. When they got to the office building, there were a couple of cars in the front of the building where the stores were located, but they recognized both of them as belonging to the folks who leased the spaces. They pulled behind the building to where the door upstairs to their offices was located. No cars were in the back parking lot.

"Let's go," Amanda said in a command voice, and they leapt from the car and rushed up to the back door, which they quickly unlocked. They immediately relocked the door, and Marcie volunteered to rush back down as soon as they saw the mail truck enter the parking lot. They hurried through their offices gathering what they needed and depositing it on Amanda's desk.

"I see the mail truck," Marcie announced glancing out the window. She ran downstairs and managed to open the door right

29

before the mail person turned the handle. The woman was a bit surprised to see Marcie standing there.

"Just thought I'd save you a few steps today," Marcie said cheerfully with a disarming smile.

"Uh, oh, thanks," the postal worker said, dumping a pile of mail in Marcie's outstretched arms. "Have a good day."

Marcie waited until the mail truck left the parking lot, then she took the mail out to Amanda's car and put it on the back seat. She went back inside and relocked the door.

"Are we ready," she asked Amanda when she got back upstairs.

Amanda was sitting behind her desk looking at something on her computer.

"We don't have time for that now. We've got to get out of here," Marcie insisted.

"Just checking to see if there was anything urgent in my emails."

"The only urgent thing right now is to hit the road."

She had just finished the sentence when there was a loud crash from the stairwell. Marcie ran to the top of the stairs and saw that the door was half broken, and a hand was reaching inside to turn the lock. That was the only way out, aside from the outside fire stairs, and the window that opened out on them had been painted shut since before Marcie got her job. They kept meaning to get Sam to have it opened, but . . . Marcie forced her mind back to the problem at hand. She rushed into Amanda's office. Amanda stood there with her eyes wide open like a deer about to become road kill.

Marcie glanced quickly around the office. "You have to stay calm and do what I say. Okay?"

Amanda nodded. Marcie told her the plan, and then she slipped into the closet on the other side of the room just as she heard heavy footsteps coming down the hall.

Through a small opening in the door Marcie saw a man in black wearing a ski mask come charging into the room carrying a large crowbar. "Where's the map," he said in a muffled voice.

"I have no idea what you are talking about," Amanda replied in a haughty tone. "And I don't appreciate your breaking in here this way."

Marcie had to admire how quickly she had regained her composure.

"Where's the map," he repeated and came across the room toward her, raising the crowbar.

"In there," Amanda said grudgingly, pointing to the open closet behind her. "On the second shelf."

The man walked into the closet, and Amanda immediately shut the door behind him. Unfortunately, neither of them knew where the key to the closet was. Marcie ran out of concealment and began pushing Amanda's heavy desk against the door. Amanda quickly came around to help her, and just in time. The desk slid into place against the door as it began to open. The intruder threw his weight against the door and the desk slowly began to slide. Marcie jammed a throw run under it.

"Let's grab our stuff and get out of here," Marcie said.

They grabbed their laptops and left the office just as the man made a second effort and the desk slid a couple more inches. They ran down the stairs. Once they were out in the parking lot, Amanda headed immediately for her car.

"Give me a minute," Marcie called, as she bent down next to the SUV that was parked next to their vehicle.

"What are you doing?" Amanda called, the fear obvious in her voice.

Marcie took out her knife and stabbed it deeply and repeatedly into the sidewall of the SUV's front tire. Then she did the same thing to the back tire. Not waiting to watch the result, she jumped into Amanda's car.

"What were you doing?" Amanda asked, as she headed out of the lot.

"Hopefully gaining us some lead time," Marcie said. She looked back and didn't see anyone coming out of the building, but knew it would only be a matter of minutes before their pursuer would be hot on their trail.

Amanda turned left on Route 1 and began to speed.

"Slow down," Marcie demanded. "If we get stopped by a cop, we will be in trouble."

Marcie looked out the back window and didn't see an SUV in hot pursuit.

"I think we're safe."

"For the time being," Amanda added.

31

"That's good enough. Let's go back to your place and make some plans," Marcie said. "Ones that will work even after we've taken a punch."

Chapter Five

"**I** think I was wrong," Marcie said slowly.

They'd been sitting on the sofa in Amanda's apartment staring into space, gradually recovering from their narrow escape.

"About what?" Amanda asked, only half paying attention as she began leafing through the mail.

"Not going to the police. I think we have to let them know what's been happening. They can't possibly blame me for what's going on, and unless they know there's a killer on the loose, this lunatic is going to hang around town until he catches up with us because he's convinced we have the map."

"We do," Amanda said.

"What are you talking about?"

Amanda held up a business envelope. "It's addressed to you, and all it has for a return address is the name Marty." She handed it to Marcie. "I think you'd better open it."

Marcie quickly tore open the envelope. Sure enough, inside was a map that appeared identical to the one that Marty had shown her in the bar that night.

"Is that the map?" Amanda asked.

"I didn't get much of a look at it when Marty showed it to me, but it sure looks like it. I wonder why he mailed it to me?"

"Probably because he had a good idea that he was being followed, and sending the map to you was the only way he could think of to keep it safe."

Marcie nodded, excited. "Now we have another option. We don't have to go to the police or live in hiding. We can go find the treasure. Once we've done that and turned it in to the authorities, the stalker will leave us alone."

"We could always give the map to the police. Maybe that would get the killer off our trail."

"Only if he found out we'd turned it in, and even then, he would probably suspect that we'd made a copy and would come after us anyway."

Amanda nodded. "I suppose you're right. We have to find the treasure. Do you think we can follow the map?"

"I think so," Marcie said, looking at the piece of paper. "I'll have to check out Jewell Island on the Internet and get a sense of the place, but Marty has given us landmarks to follow. We should be able to find the treasure."

"Okay. Why don't you do some computer research, while I go have a chat with Richard? I still think we need him to come along, don't you?"

"Now more than ever, since we don't have Marty to help us anymore," Marcie said with a note of sadness in her voice. "But can you talk him into going?"

Amanda gave an elegant shrug. "Usually he'll do what I ask him to do, but getting him away from that hotel is a challenge. I'd better trot over there right now and talk to him. We have to find that treasure before the killer finds us."

Marcie nodded and turned on her computer, while Amanda picked up her handbag and headed for the door.

"Oh, by the way, " Marcie called out. "If Richard has a gun, tell him to bring it along."

• • • •

AMANDA STOOD IN THE doorway of Richard's office and watched her sometime fiancé. He was focused so intently on his computer that he wasn't even aware that she was standing there. The young woman working at the front desk had smiled and waved her through to the back offices, saying something about getting the boss to take a break. When he was so focused, there was something vulnerable and adorable about him. Amanda smiled to herself and wanted to rush up and put her arms around him. But she resisted the impulse. Ever since she had ended their engagement or at least put it on hold, she was reluctant to be spontaneously affectionate for fear that it would encourage Richard into thinking she wanted them to go back to the way things had been.

Finally, Richard looked up and saw her in the doorway. He smiled. "Hi there. I'm just working on some advertising."

"Aren't you always?" Amanda tried to keep her tone light, but she could tell by the expression on his face that Richard had taken it as a criticism.

"It's one of the things you have to do when you run a hotel," he replied.

"Of course." Amanda walked into the room and took a chair in front of his desk. "Look, there's something I want to discuss with you. I'm not sure you can take time off from work, but I'd like you to at least consider it."

"What did you have in mind?" he asked with a guarded smile.

Amanda gave him a concise summary of what had happened so far regarding the pirate map. When she was done, Amanda expected him to immediately launch into a rant on how foolish she and Marcie had been to get involved in this case in the first place. However, he surprised her by sitting there quietly for several seconds as if absorbing the information.

"You know, this is the first time you've asked for my help in one of your investigations."

We've never been so desperate before, Amanda thought, but decided saying that would be undiplomatic.

"I didn't think you were interested. Does that mean you'll help us?"

"My instincts tell me that this whole idea is crazy and foolish. It's just the kind of thing that Marcie would get involved in, but you usually have better sense."

Amanda ignored the criticism. "Well, Marcie can't do it alone. In fact, even the two of us don't have enough muscle to lug out a treasure chest."

"If there is one."

Amanda shrugged. "If there isn't, we'll have spent a nice day on the water. Are you willing to come along?"

Something flashed in Richard's eyes. She could tell whether it was fear or the love of a challenge.

"Do you really want me to help?"

Amanda nodded, wondering if she was on the road to further complicating her personal life.

"Okay. I agree with you that the police might not be much help, and the best thing is to find this treasure before the killer finds you. Fortunately, I'm not incredibly busy right now. I can take a couple of days off to help. I'll call up to Portland this afternoon and arrange for our transportation out to Jewell Island. We probably want to go as soon as possible. Is tomorrow morning all right with you?"

"That would be fine," Amanda said, her head still spinning from the way Richard had quickly taken control. "Are you sure you want to do this?"

Richard smiled. "I know I don't exactly give the impression of being a man of action, but I'm not completely incapable of getting things done."

"I know you're very efficient at running the hotel . . ."

"This is different, I agree. However, organizational skills carry over to the accomplishment of any goal. Do you and Marcie have the gear you'll need to hike around the island?"

"We can buy anything that we need."

Richard frowned. "Don't go travelling around town more than you have to. Remember, there is a killer out there looking for you."

Amanda nodded. "Marcie said I should ask whether you have a gun."

"I have a handgun that's registered to me. I keep it in the hotel just in case."

"I think you should bring it."

"Why would we need it? The killer doesn't have a map, so how will he be able to follow us?"

"We don't know how long he was following Marty. He may know that Marty went out to Jewell Island, but just not know exactly where the treasure is."

Richard furrowed is brow. "That does change things a bit, doesn't it? Okay, I'll bring the automatic."

"Do you know how to use it?"

"I went out to a firing range when I first got it to familiarize myself with how it worked. But I haven't taken any target practice in a couple of years. I suppose I could hit something if it was close enough, but I'd rather not."

"You and me both," Amanda agreed.

"Give me a call tonight, and I'll fill you in on the travel details. We should probably take my SUV."

Amanda stood up and Richard did as well. After an awkward moment, Amanda stepped forward and gave Richard a kiss on the cheek.

"Thanks, I appreciate the help."

Richard smiled gently and nodded.

36

Chapter Six

Marcie looked up as Amanda came in the door.

"How'd it go with Richard?" Marcie asked.

"Much to my surprise, he agreed to go along. In fact I believe he's even excited at the idea of having an adventure. He's got more on the ball than I ever gave him credit for."

Marcie smiled. "Is that any way to talk about your sometime fiancé?"

"I know. It sounds bad. But sometimes he drives me crazy with the amount of time he spends thinking about that hotel of his."

"You spend a lot of time working on the magazine."

"I suppose. Maybe Richard and I both need to lighten up. Anyway, he's going to take charge of arranging for our transportation out to Jewell Island."

"Did you ask him about the gun?"

"He's got one and is going to bring it along."

"Good. I've been reviewing satellite pictures of the island and comparing them to Marty's map. I think I've got a pretty good idea of where he claims the treasure is. Of course, nothing looks the same on the ground as it does from the air or on a map. But with a bit of luck, we actually might be able to find it."

"Do you think we need to bring a lot of equipment to get the treasure off the island?"

"Marty must have done all the digging that needs to be done. After all, he had a coin from the treasure in his pocket when he met with me. But I have an old army surplus entrenching tool from my camping days in my car. I'll bring that along in my backpack. I already have all the clothes I need."

"I'm going to need a backpack. I don't have one of those."

"You live in Maine, and you don't have a backpack. What do you have?"

"A suitcase," Amanda said defensively. "It's always been adequate in the past."

Marcie sighed. "Okay, this should only take us a day, so you can put a change of socks and whatever else you want to bring in my pack. Do you have shoes? Something other than pumps or high heels."

"Of course," Amanda said. She went into her bedroom closet, and returned in a few minutes with a pair of pink trainers. "I wear these when I go to the gym."

"Very cute. But it looks to me like some of our walking will be off road. You might need a pair that are a bit more rugged. We don't have time for you to break in a pair of hiking boots, but maybe we can find some low-cut hiking shoes that will give you sturdier soles than those trainers."

"That means we'll have to go shopping. We might run into the killer."

"What are the odds? We'll go out to that mall with all the discount stores. There's a store there that will have the shoes you need."

"Okay. Let me just put on the clothes I plan to wear tomorrow to see how I look."

"I don't think you have to worry about the outfit working together. No one is going to see you out in the woods except the wild animals."

"Richard will."

"He'd think you looked good in a burlap sack."

"I'll just be a minute," Amanda said disappearing into her bedroom.

She returned ten minutes later dressed in a long sleeved plaid shirt and a pair of cargo pants with a sweatshirt tied fashionably around her neck.

"I'm ready."

Marcie nodded, stifling the comment that some people must think walking in the forest was the same a walking down the runway at a fashion show. She carefully folded the map and slipped it in the pocket of her jacket. After some prodding, Amanda put a change of underwear and socks in Marcie's backpack.

They drove out of Amanda's parking lot and turned right onto Route 1. It was only a few miles to the mall of discount stores. Marcie talked some more about what she had learned from Marty's map, and why she thought they would find the treasure without too much difficulty.

"Do you know why I want to find the treasure?" she suddenly asked Amanda.

"I would imagine so that you can write a really good story."

"Well, of course, but do you know why this story means a lot to me?"

Amanda shrugged. "I thought they all did."

"This one is particularly important because I want to make sure that Marty isn't forgotten. I got the impression from our brief conversation that he felt he had never amounted to much in life and that this treasure was going to be his chance to really be somebody. Whoever killed Marty took that away from him. But even if Marty will never know it, I intend to see that he is remembered."

"I certainly agree with that," Amanda said softly.

They pulled into the parking lot.

"Park over there," Marcie said, pointing at a store with a phony log cabin façade.

"That's the place we're going?" Amanda asked doubtfully.

"I know it doesn't look like much, but they have everything for camping and hiking."

Amanda parked and they went inside. She was surprised to see how large the store was. It seemed like a warehouse filled with items, most of which she could barely identify.

"The clothes are toward the front of the store. They have kayaks and camping gear in the back. The shoes are along the right wall," Marcie said. "I'm going to pick up a couple more pairs of socks. Let's not take all day. We don't want to be out in public more than we have to be."

Amanda nodded and headed for the shoe section. She soon a found a pair of hiking shoes that fit and were stylish enough to be acceptable. A good thing, because the store seemed woefully understaffed. That was the problem with discount stores she thought, there was never anyone around to help you. On her way to the cash register, she passed by a rack of shirts that were advertised as being especially for hiking. They were made of a fabric that wicked away moisture and had sleeves that could be worn down or rolled up and secured at half-length. She picked out a color that went well with the shoes and the hiking slacks she had just found, and then headed for the cash register in front. She expected to see Marcie standing there impatiently tapping her foot, but no one was around. In fact it took several minutes before the young woman handling the cash register appeared.

After Amanda paid, she began drifting toward the back of the store, looking for her friend. She was about to browse through a rack of hiking shorts, when a hand tightened around her arm. She felt a point pressing into her back.

Before she could turn around a voice said. "That's a knife you feel. Just keep walking toward the back of the store if you don't want to get hurt. Where's that friend of yours?"

"I don't know," Amanda stammered.

"Which one of you has the map?"

"She does," Amanda said quickly. She knew she was dropping Marcie into a world of pain, but if she lied and said she had it, he might quickly kill her to get it.

"Keep walking until we find that friend of yours," he said, poking her in the back again. Amanda found that the repeated jabbing with the knife was making her angry rather than frightened.

"Where is she?" he asked pulling harder on her arm.

"Probably over by the camping gear," she said, just for something to say to stop his physical abuse. *Where was Marcie? It was only a matter of time before, this killer decided to stab her and look for Marcie on his own.*

They walked toward the back of the store past the kayaks and tents.

"Okay, where is she? If you've been lying to . . ."

The point of the knife disappeared from Amanda's back, and she was shoved to one side as a body fell to the floor next to her. She turned and saw Marcie standing there with a hatchet in her hand.

Amanda's eyes opened wide. "Did you kill him?"

"I used the blunt side, but I'm already regretting it," she said as the man started to slowly crawl to his knees. "Let's get out of here."

The two women turned and ran for the exit. Amanda noted that there wasn't even a sales clerk by the cash register to watch them tear out of the store. *We could be shoplifting a canoe, and no one would notice. Poor security,* she thought.

They ran to the car and Amanda pulled out of the space without a glance behind. She sped toward the exit from the mall.

"Back to my place," Amanda said.

"Wait! Let's think about this. Keep driving, but go somewhere else."

"Where?"

"Just cruise around at random."

Amanda frowned. She didn't like not having a destination. "Why can't we go back to my place?"

"Think about it," Marcie said. "What are the odds that this guy happened to come upon us in the store?"

"How else could he have found us?"

"He was staking out your condo and followed us here."

"But how . . ."

"He went online and looked up the magazine. That would give him both of our names. Are you listed in the phone book?"

"I don't know. I suppose so."

"Either he found a phone book and got your address or he researched your name on line. I bet somewhere it gives your home address. Nothing is really private anymore."

"So what do we do?" Amanda asked frantically.

"We drive around for a while to make sure he isn't following us, then we go to Richard's hotel. That creep won't know to look there. We should be safe until tomorrow. Do you have all the clothes you'll need?"

"My underwear is in your backpack. My shoes and an extra shirt and pair of slacks are in the bag."

"Extra clothes. You really are going to take your turn carrying my pack." Marcie paused for a moment. "It's a shame really."

"What is?" Amanda asked.

"With everything going on, I never got to buy my extra socks."

41

Chapter Seven

Richard knocked on the driver's side window. When the window rolled down, he said, "Hello, Amanda." He glanced across to the passenger's seat. "Hello, Marcie," he said more grudgingly.

Marcie gave him a big smile.

"Why did you call and ask me to meet you out here in the hotel parking lot?" he asked.

Amanda looked over at Marcie, as if to say that it was her job to provide an explanation.

"We think the killer has found out where Amanda lives. He already knows where I live, so the only place where we can be safe is here."

Richard looked out at the busy road behind them, as several questions seemed to go through his mind. "Okay, drive the car around back and park it. Come inside through the rear door. I'll arrange a room for you without having you officially check in. That way your presence here will be a complete secret."

They did as he indicated, and a few minutes later he held the back door open for them as they carried their gear down the hall. They followed Richard and soon found themselves in a large suite that looked out on the wooded mountain in back of the hotel.

"This should be adequate for now," Richard announced as they entered the room.

"It's huge," Marcie said.

"Yeah, it's a VIP suite, and we hardly ever rent it. Since you aren't officially registered, no maid will be coming around. So no one will know that you're here. You can leave whatever stuff you don't need for the trip in the room and pick it up when we get back. Now tell me how you found out that he knew your address," he said to Amanda.

Amanda told him about the events in the camping store. When she got to the part where the killer had a knife to her back, Richard shook his head.

"This is getting too dangerous. We should call the police and let them handle it."

"I'm sure Amanda's already explained why that won't work," Marcie said. "The police already half-believe that I killed Marty and stole the map. If I show up with the map now and try to tell that there's a murderer following us, what do you think is going to happen?"

"They'll bring you in for questioning and take the map, so you'll be off the hook," he replied.

Marcie smiled. "Only in the days before copying machines. The killer will think I made a copy first, and he'll plan to get hold of it. We'll be back where we are right now only he'll have a better idea where we are."

"Couldn't you describe this guy to the police?" Richard asked.

"Did you get a good look at him?" Marcie asked Amanda.

She shook her head. "He stood behind me most of the time, and he was face down after Marcie hit him. All I know is that he's around six feet tall and thin."

"And I don't know much more than she does except that he had dark hair. When you're hitting a guy on the back of the head with a hatchet, you don't get much chance to draw a sketch."

"Okay, okay," Richard said, rubbing his face with his hands. "We stick with the plan. You two stay hidden tonight, and we set out tomorrow for Jewell Island. I've contacted the owner of a ship who sails out of Portland for Jewell Island on a regular basis. He can take us on short notice because it's the middle of the week. Once the summer is over, most of the tourists only go out there on the weekends. I put it all on my credit card, so your names wouldn't be involved."

"The magazine will cover your costs," Amanda said.

"I'm not worried about that," Richard said, his brow furrowing. "My concern is that we all survive this little adventure."

"You can't find a pirate treasure without taking risks," Marcie said, flopping down in an upholstered chair.

Richard stared at her for a moment, as if she exemplified everything he didn't agree with.

"I'll personally bring you some lunch in an hour," he said, turning on his heel. "Don't leave the room."

"Did I offend him?" Marcie asked once the door had closed.

Amanda gave her a small smile and shook her head. "I think the fact that you get a high out of putting your life in danger is what bothers him. He's the kind of guy who wears a belt and suspenders at the same time just to be sure."

Marcie laughed. "At least he came through with the boat." She paused for a moment as if unsure whether to continue. "Is that why you aren't engaged to him any more, because he's too careful?"

"I'm not exactly madcap myself, but sometimes he makes my skin itch with all his cautiousness. He acts like he's seventy instead of thirty-five. I'm not ready to be that old just yet."

"Well, one good thing about guys like Richard."

"What's that?"

"They usually don't forget to bring lunch."

• • • •

AS PROMISED, RICHARD returned an hour later with lunch. He had a thick roast beef wrap for Marcie, who never shied away from red meat, and a vegetarian wrap for Amanda.

After handing out the food, he stood at one end of the room, while they ate.

"I checked out the parking lot from the upstairs front windows," he announced. "There's no sign of a suspicious SUV. So I guess you were able to give him the slip. Since there are probably thirty hotels and bed and breakfasts still open this late in the season, I doubt he's going to check each one carefully. Even if he did drive by here, he'd never see your car parked in the back lot."

"That's great. We appreciate your help," Amanda said, giving him a grateful smile.

"Are you ready to go tomorrow or is there anything you need?"

"I've got all the clothes I need, so I'm fine," Amanda said, glancing over at Marcie, who had her mouth full of beef and just gave a thumbs up.

Richard turned to Marcie. "I need to know if you'll be able to follow that map directly to the treasure. The Captain has given us time parameters. He can drop us off on the island at ten o'clock, and he'll return for us at three. So we can't randomly wander around the island looking for the treasure. Even a small island like Jewell would take lots of time to explore if we aren't certain where to go."

"I believe I've got the map figured out. If I can find a few landmarks, we shouldn't have much difficulty locating the treasure sooner rather than later."

44

Richard nodded. "We'll be depending on it."

"How did you find this particular captain?" asked Amanda.

"He's the only one who goes out to Jewell Island during the week in the off-season. There are several others who take tourists out there on the weekends, but they only go out during the week in the summer. We need to meet him at the dock by eight-thirty, so we'll have to leave here by seven o'clock tomorrow morning. I'll bring you breakfast at six. The kitchen isn't officially open that early, but the chef will whip up something for you."

"What about dinner tonight?" Marcie asked between bites of her wrap.

"There's small private dining room down the hall from the main one, and we can eat there. Since you weren't followed here, that should be safe enough."

"And what do we do for the rest of the afternoon?" Marcie continued.

Richard shrugged. "You've got Wi-Fi here. Work on magazine stuff or whatever you would normally do."

Giving them a quick nod, he left the room.

"Not one for a lot of small talk is he?" Marcie said.

Amanda laughed. "He's in command mode. Right now he's Mr. Hotel Manager. I guess he figures organizing a treasure hunt is the same as setting up a wedding banquet."

Marcie nodded. "Let's hope he's right."

Chapter Eight

The next morning Marcie looked out the window of the black SUV Richard was driving from the hotel to Portland. Although feeling a bit nervous in the early morning darkness, she was happy to finally be on the way. Yesterday afternoon and evening had dragged as Amanda and she had finished up the details of the next issue of the magazine, trying to concentrate on editorial questions, while their minds kept drifting to Jewell Island and pirate treasure. True to his word, Richard had set them up in a small guest dining room in the back of the hotel. He didn't eat with them, begging off because he had lots of hotel work to do before tomorrow's departure.

Amanda had only picked at her food, and even Marcie had eaten sparingly, whether due to nerves or the lack of activity during the day, she wasn't sure. Although Marcie had some reservations about such a dangerous undertaking, she couldn't see any way out of the situation they were in. Only by finding the treasure would they cease being a target for Marty's killer. She half suspected that the murderer was long gone after the confrontation in the sporting goods store, but there was no way to be sure. Certainty would only come once she had the gold doubloons in her hand.

They took an indirect route along country roads, staying alert to the possibility of being followed. But in the early morning the roads were empty, and there was no sign of a tail. They drove into South Portland and eastward toward the docks. When they reached the water, Richard pulled into a parking facility, and they unloaded the SUV. Marcie and Richard put on their backpacks.

"I feel like a freeloader not carrying anything," Amanda said.

"Don't worry about it, there will be plenty for you to carry once we find the treasure," Marcie replied.

"*If* we find the treasure," Richard said.

"Don't be such a downer," Amanda said, giving him a smile.

"Yeah, the most important thing about a treasure hunt is that you have to stay optimistic," Marcie added.

Richard gave both the women dubious looks.

46

They walked along the dock with Richard taking the lead. "The captain said that the boat was in one of the middle slips."

"What's the boat's name?" Marcie asked.

"The Serendipity."

"I like that name. A fortunate coincidence is just what we need on this project."

"There it is," Richard said suddenly, pointing up ahead.

Marcie was surprised to see that The Serendipity was not the usual wide-bottomed ferry style boat, but instead looked like a medium-sized motor yacht with a row boat attached in the back. They walked along the dock and out to where the boat was moored. They stood by the boat, but no one appeared to be on board.

"Hello," Richard called out.

There was no response.

"Ahoy!" Marcie called out loudly.

A head popped up from the front hatch, and slowly a short chubby man pulled himself fully into view. He appeared to be in late middle age and had a stubbly gray beard.

"Are you Captain Adams?" Richard asked.

"That I am," the man said with a broad smile. "I take it that you're the folks who want to go to Jewell Island."

"That we are," Marcie said, getting into the swing of things.

"Well, come on board," he said, reaching out a hand to help each of them onto the deck.

"When will we be leaving?" Richard asked, right after shaking hands with the captain.

"I'm ready whenever you are," the captain said. "You can stow your gear below deck. There's coffee and some donuts down there for those who want them."

"Sounds good," Marcie said with enthusiasm.

The captain smiled. "It's fine to have one good eater on board. But be careful, the trip across can be a little rough, and we don't want people hanging over the rail."

"I've been on lots of small boats before. I won't have any problem," Marcie said.

Richard and Amanda looked less certain.

The captain jumped onto the dock, untied the ropes from the bollards, and, with surprising nimbleness for a heavy man, leapt back on board. A few minutes later the rumble of the boat's motor started and they slowly pulled away from the dock. The three passengers went below and placed their gear in a rack along the side of the boat. Marcie made a beeline for the urn of coffee and selected a powdered sugar donut.

She looked at her two friends. "Don't you want anything?"

"I think I'll play it safe," Amanda said. Richard looked around a bit nervously and didn't bother to answer, as the boat quickly began to rock.

Marcie went back on deck and up a few steps to the forward cabin. She stood next to the captain, who was sitting on a chair behind the wheel. He glanced over at her.

"Find what you needed?" he said with a smile as she gobbled her donut. Marcie nodded happily.

"I appreciate the food. We left early, and it's been a while since breakfast. So are we heading across Casco Bay?"

He nodded. "We'll head east southeast and go between Peaks Island and Fort Levett. From there we go slightly northeast to Jewell. We should be there is a little over an hour.

"Do you take a lot of people out there?"

"During the summer months, I usually take between five or ten over there most days. Not many folks heading out that way now that the summer's over, but I'll still get bookings on the weekends."

"What do people do there?"

"Walk along the trails, check out the old fire control towers and the gun emplacements, wade in the Punchbowl, that's a tidal pool." He paused and glanced at her. "Don't you have anything planned?"

Marcie realized that she had never stopped to work on their cover story as innocent tourists rather than treasure hunters.

"We'll walk along the trail from Cocktail Bay," she said, remembering one of the names from her map. "Then wander along Smugglers' trail."

"Yeah, being that the island is only a mile long, you really can't get lost. Just watch out for the giant raccoons."

"Giant raccoons?"

"Yep. They're fearless. If you've got any food in your packs and leave them unguarded for a few minutes, they'll tear them apart to get at it. They're big suckers, too, the size of a bear cub."

Marcie shivered. She didn't like raccoons even at the best of times. She thought their little masks made them look larcenous. Plus, they carried disease and could be vicious. Wild giant raccoons sounded even worse. She debated whether to tell Amanda, who might refuse to get off the boat at the thought of any large wild animals, and decided that the less said the better. She stood next to the captain for the next half hour and watched as he navigated around the last of the islands then headed directly for Jewell. She hoped that her interpretation of Marty's map was correct and that they would find the site of the treasure without too much difficulty. But soon she put her concerns behind her and focused on the trip.

"Here we are," Captain Adams said twenty minutes later, as they sailed into a small cove. "This is Cocktail Cove. A lot of partying goes on here at night in the summer, but it's dead quiet this time of year."

"We're here," Marcie called down to the others. A minute later Amanda and Richard appeared.

"Looks pretty peaceful," Richard said.

"Yep, you're the only ones on the island as far as I know. Do you need any food to take with you? It's all part of the service."

"We're all set," Marcie said. Richard had seen to it that they had water and sandwiches before leaving the hotel.

Amanda stared at the two hundred feet of water that separated them from shore. "How do we get the boat closer to the land?" she asked.

"We can't get any closer. There isn't anywhere for the boat to dock. We'll have to go the rest of the way by rowboat. Follow me."

He led them to the rear of the boat and pointed to a ladder that led down to the rowboat attached at the rear. "Just climb down that ladder and step into the rowboat. Try not to tip her over," he said with a smile.

"I don't know . . .?" Amanda said apprehensively.

"I'll go first," Marcie said. She climbed backwards down the ladder and stepped cautiously onto the bottom of the boat. It shifted slightly under her feet, but she made her way to a seat at the far end and settled in.

Richard went next. He stumbled slightly, but with a helping hand from Marcie, quickly regained his balance. He remained standing and helped Amanda onto the boat, which she did with considerable grace. Marcie figured that all that ballet practice had paid off. The captain hopped aboard with practiced skill.

49

"Everyone ready?" he asked with a broad smile, grabbing the oars and beginning to row. In a few minutes the rowboat was being pulled up on the sandy beach. "If you hop out the bow end, you won't get your feet wet," he said.

Once they were all on shore, he turned to them and smiled. "Now you all have a good time. I'll row back and wait in the boat offshore. But don't get lost, and please be back by three o'clock. I'd like to make it back into port before sunset. The trip is more interesting after it gets dark."

They all nodded and agreed. Richard gave Captain Adams a hand at pushing the rowboat off the beach.

When the group was gathered, Amanda said, "Okay, where do we go now?"

"Let's follow this path for a little while," Marcie said.

"Is that the way we want to go?" asked Richard.

"Not exactly, but I want us to get into the woods and out of sight before I take out the compass and the map, just in case anyone is watching."

Amanda looked around. "I don't see a soul except for us and the captain."

"You can't be too sure," Marcie replied, leading away along the path toward the trees.

They walked deeper into the woods. The path became narrower, and soon they were going single file. Marcie took out her map and a compass.

"We follow this trail for another fifty yards, then it looks like we take a path off to the right."

"Do you have any idea where we're going?" asked Richard.

"We're heading in the direction of the Military Reservation, but we don't go nearly that far."

They walked for another five minutes when Marcie stopped and began looking into the distance.

"What are you looking for?" Amanda asked.

"You see that tower."

"The one that looks like the top of an observation deck?"

"Yeah. That's part of the World War II gun batteries that were built to defend the coast of Maine. As I understand the map, we turn right somewhere around here and head toward the center of the island."

"I don't see any path going that way," Richard said.

Marcie said nothing. She began walking ahead with a careful eye on the right side of the path. Suddenly she stopped. "I wonder why that bush looks dead?" she said, pointing to a brown patch in the bank of green foliage along the side of the trail. She went over and began to pull on the branches.

"Be careful," Amanda warned, "it could be poison oak or something."

Marcie ignored her. After another few minutes of effort, the dead bush pulled free, and she tossed it out onto the path. A narrow trail was revealed.

"Someone put this here to conceal the path we need to follow," Marcie said. "I'll bet it was Marty. He didn't want anyone to stumble on the treasure."

"It's been hidden for hundreds of years. Why would he expect anyone to just find it now?" Richard asked.

"Because by uncovering the cave, Marty probably made it easier to find," Marcie answered. "Let's go," she said, moving forward.

Amanda shrugged and waved her hand ineffectually at the little flying bugs starting to surround her face.

"I told you to put on some bug spray," Richard said.

"I'm allergic," Amanda replied, starting to trudge after Marcie. "You know I keep feeling like someone is watching us."

"Probably a squirrel," Marcie replied.

They went several hundred yards down the trail, where they came to a clearing.

"Let's stop here for a moment," Marcie said, sitting on a fallen tree trunk. She opened her pack and took out a sandwich. She handed one to Amanda.

"Are you hungry already?" said Amanda. "It's only ten o'clock."

"And we ate at six," Marcie replied.

"She's got a point," Richard said. He opened his pack and took out his lunch as well. Reluctantly, Amanda followed suit.

"Where do we go from here?" Richard asked.

"Looks to me like we go on this trail for another eighth of a mile. We'll come to a clearing, and there should be an opening into a cave. That's where the treasure is hidden."

"Will we be able to find the opening to the cave?" Amanda asked.

"According to Marty's map, it says there will be a cleft in the rock."

"What does . . .?"

A loud rustling came from the bush nearest Marcie. She jumped to her feet and backed away as the largest raccoon she'd ever seen came ambling out into the clearing. Although she desperately wanted to turn and run, Marcie kept her eye on the creature as she cautiously bent down and picked up her sandwich from where it had fallen. She shoved it into her backpack. The raccoon moved toward her, showing no signs of fear.

"Let me get a shot at it," Richard said. He already had his gun out of his jacket pocket and was moving in the direction of the animal.

Marcie put up her hand. "I don't think we should. A shot might alert Captain Adams, and he might call the Coast Guard. Also, we could end up in a lot of trouble for shooting the island wildlife."

Marcie picked up a large branch and suddenly ran at the raccoon, shouting loudly. Looking singularly unimpressed, the raccoon turned and slowly waddled back into the woods.

"Did you see the size of that thing?" said Richard.

Amanda quickly began shoving her food into Marcie's pack. "So much for al fresco dining. I'll wait to eat until I can sit comfortably inside a restaurant tonight."

"Yeah, we may as well move on," Marcie agreed.

They headed down the trail, looking carefully to each side, afraid that at any moment a giant raccoon might jump out at them.

"I wouldn't want to spend the night out here," Amanda said. "I already feel like I'm being watched."

"That's your imagination, and don't worry, we won't be out here tonight. We'll either find the treasure in the next hour or we won't, either way we leave," Marcie assured her.

Marcie was just starting to wonder if she had misread the map when they finally came into the clearing. They glanced around, looking for a cave. One side of the clearing was composed of rock face, and at the far right end was a pile of stones and dirt. She examined the wall in that area.

"I don't see any cave," Richard said, coming over to stand next to Marcie.

"No, but somebody has been working here recently. This pile of dirt looks pretty recent. It had to come from somewhere," Marcie responded. "Stands to reason, Marty wouldn't have piled stuff up right near the opening to the cave. That would be too much of a giveaway."

Marcie turned to look behind her. "Where's Amanda?" she asked.

"She was here a moment ago," Richard said.

They looked around the clearing, but there was no sign of her.

"Where could she have gone?" Richard asked, panic seeping into his voice.

Marcie walked down to the other end of the rock face, just as Amanda reappeared from behind a bush.

"Hi, guys," Amanda said cheerfully. "I think I found the cave."

"You scared me half to death disappearing like that," Richard said.

"Sorry, but I spotted the opening and went inside to see if it was really a cave. It's dark as can be in there and I didn't have a flashlight, so it took me a few moments to find my way out again. C'mon, I'll show you."

They got flashlights out of their backpacks and went with Amanda to look behind the bush where she had disappeared. Barely visible behind the foliage was a split in the rock wall.

"Look at this," Marcie said, pointing to what appeared to be recent scars on the rocks. "I'll bet this had been covered with rocks, and Marty dug it out. It must have taken him a while to remove all that debris."

They snapped on their flashlights and, turning sideways, slipped through the narrow opening. Once they were through, the tunnel widened in front of them. They had gone about thirty steps when Marcie, who was leading the way, stopped in her tracks, and directed the beam of her flashlight toward the wall of the cave.

"Are they what I think they are?" she asked.

Amanda and Richard stopped. "They look like bones," said Amanda in a faint voice.

"Could be the bones of anything," Richard said. "Probably animals have used this cave."

"I don't think those are the bones of just any animal," Marcie said. "Look over here." She directed her flashlight a few feet further into the cave revealing two skulls that were definitely human. "They look kind of yellow. I bet they've been here a long time."

"Probably Captain Kidd killed the members of his crew who helped him to move the treasure, so they wouldn't be able to reveal where it was hidden," said Richard.

"Some employer," Marcie muttered.

"Let's keep moving and find this treasure and get out of here. This place gives me the creeps," Amanda said.

A few yards further and they came to a small chamber. At the far end there was a stone overhang and something was sticking out of the wall a few feet above the floor. Marcie walked closer and directed her light on the wall.

"There's a wooden chest half buried in the wall," she said excitedly. "It looks like the top has a hole in it."

The others came over next to her. "Look at that," Richard said, eyeing the gold coins that were visible through the hole. "There must be a fortune there."

"Will the chest come out of the wall?" Amanda asked.

Richard grabbed one end and gave a hard pull. "It won't budge. The rock around it is firmly in place."

"I don't think my entrenching tool is going to be of much use," Marcie said.

"We need a pickax," Richard said.

"Maybe I can help," a voice said from the shadows behind them.

Chapter Nine

A tall, thin man in his fifties stepped into the light. He seized Amanda from behind and held a gun to her head. "Now unless you want blondie here to have a fatal accident, I would suggest that you take that gun out of your pocket, that I know you have from watching you back in the clearing, and put it on the ground."

Richard reached into his jacket pocket and placed the automatic on the floor of the cave. The man released Amanda and stepped forward to pick up the gun. Amanda immediately leapt onto his back. Before Richard could help her, the man threw her off and Amanda crashed into the wall of the cave and crumpled to the ground. Before Richard or Marcie could make a move, the man again had the gun pointed at them. He picked up Richard's gun and put it in the pocket of his windbreaker.

"That was stupid. If either of you two is planning to do anything similar, remember I don't care who I have to kill to get that treasure."

"You mean like you killed Marty," Marcie said.

"Yeah, he was stupid, as well, and wouldn't tell me where the map was."

"It was his map."

"It was *my* map!" the man shouted. "I'm Scott Winston. He got it from *my* father. He sucked up to my father until he gave it to him when he died."

"So you're the son who disappeared, and never did anything for his father when he was sick."

The man waved the gun at Marcie. "It seems that you're as stupid as blondie. You know, I don't need all three of you to help me carry the treasure."

Marcie decided it was a good time to keep her mouth shut.

Richard ignored the man with the gun and walked over to Amanda who was struggling to get up from the floor. He put his arm around her waist to help her up. Then he reached into his backpack and got out a bottle of water. He gave her a drink, then poured some water out in his hand and began to rub in on her forehead.

"Feeling better?" Richard asked.

She nodded, but looked over apprehensively at the man with the gun.

"Very sweet," the man said to Richard. "The next time you move without permission, you're dead."

The man pointed his flashlight at the far wall of the cave. "See that pickaxe over there?" he said to Richard. "Take it and see if you can get that chest out."

The man backed up to the wall behind, so he could watch all three of them at the same time.

Richard began chipping away at the wall the treasure chest was embedded in.

"How did you get over to the island without the boat captain seeing you?" Marcie asked.

"I came over by kayak yesterday. I knew the treasure was on Jewell Island, and I figured you'd come looking for it as soon as you could. So I decided to camp out near the cove until you all showed up. It didn't take a skilled tracker to follow the three of you after that."

"You'll never get this gold back to shore on a kayak," Marcie said.

He laughed. "You'd be surprised how much a kayak can carry. It might ride a little low in the water, but don't worry, I'll get it all back to land. I'm motivated."

Richard continued working on the wall. When he got tired, the man told Marcie to take over. She wasn't as good at it as Richard, but she could see that they were making progress. A large area at the top and both sides of the chest had been hollowed out. Pretty soon, she guessed, the chest would come loose.

"You two," the man said to Richard and Marcie. "Get on either side of the chest and start to pull. It should be ready to come out by now."

Richard and Marcie got on either side of the chest and began to pull. Marcie could feel it begin to give.

"It's starting to move, but I'm not strong enough to budge it," she said.

"Get out of the way," the man shouted impatiently, elbowing Marcie out of the way to take her place. He waved the gun at the two women. "Don't get any funny ideas, I can kill you before you move."

Marcie and Amanda both stood behind Richard, while the man took the other side.

"Now pull!" he shouted to Richard.

The two men grunted as they pulled as hard as they could on the end of the treasure chest.

"Again. I can feel it moving," the man shouted.

The two men resumed pulling. Slowly, with a grinding sound, the treasure chest began to come out of the wall.

"Keep pulling," he shouted.

Suddenly there was a loud cracking and the shelf of rock above the treasure chest began to crumble. Amanda quickly reached forward, locked her arms around Richard's waist, and pulled him away from the treasure chest. They stumbled backwards, barely missed by large boulders raining down from overhead. Scott Winston looked up at the last minute and saw the rocks coming down toward him, but he froze, as if unwilling to let go of the treasure even to save his life. In a matter of seconds he was buried under rocks. Marcie, in the meantime, had seized Richard's side of the treasure chest and managed to pull it in her direction before a rock struck her on the arm.

The cave was filled with a suffocating cloud of dust. The three of them slowly made their way to the front of the cave where they coughed, struggling to catch their breath.

"Are you all right?" Amanda finally asked Richard.

"Thanks to you. If you hadn't pulled me out of there, I don't know what would have happened."

Amanda reached forward and wiped some of the dirt off of his face. They looked over at Marcie, who was sitting quietly.

"Are you okay?" Amanda asked.

"Pretty good, but I think my arm may be broken."

Amanda moved across to touch her arm.

"Better leave it be," Marcie said quickly. "One of those rocks hit it. It's probably not a bad break."

"Does it hurt?" Amanda asked.

"Not yet. But it probably will start to soon. Look we've got to get that treasure out of there."

"But isn't it a crime scene?" asked Amanda.

"Actually, it's an accident scene or maybe the site of Captain Kidd's revenge But if we don't get that gold out of there, it could be gone by the next time we come back," Marcie replied.

"Can we even reach the treasure chest?" Richard asked.

"I pulled it over to one side, just as the rocks fell. I think that with a little use of the pickaxe, we can pull it out of the pile of rubble."

They slowly went back into the cave. The dust had died down a bit, and they were able to survey the damage. On the far side, away from them, was Scott Winston. His body was covered with rocks, his sightless eyes staring at the ceiling.

"He could have escaped if he'd just let go of the gold," Richard said.

"Some people can never let go," Marcie said.

"I'm not sure that I would have, if Amanda hadn't pulled me away," Richard said, glancing gratefully at Amanda.

She smiled back. "That looks to me like one end of the treasure chest sticking out over here, so maybe we can get the gold after all."

Carefully using the pickaxe, Richard was soon able to uncover the treasure chest. He and Amanda tried to lift it, and carry the chest toward the front of the cave. But it was too heavy, and they could barely drag it a few yards before they gave up.

"That must weigh well over a hundred pounds. We'll never be able to carry it all the way back to the boat," Richard said.

Using her good arm, Marcie reached into her backpack. "I brought along some laundry bags. Divide the gold up into these, and don't make any one of them too heavy. Amanda, you can carry one. I can carry one with my good arm. And Richard, you can probably carry two. I brought four bags, so that should probably do it."

"You think of everything," Amanda said.

"Well, I did think walking back to the boat carrying a treasure chest might look a bit suspicious."

"You think carrying four laundry bags filled with Spanish doubloons will look normal?" Amanda asked.

"It's all relative."

When they had divided the gold into four bags, they glanced around them.

"I wish I didn't have to leave my gun behind," said Richard. "The police probably aren't going to be happy about that."

"It's buried under a ton of rock," Marcie said. "It'll be safe until they retrieve the guy's body." She checked her watch. "We'd better start back if we don't want to miss the boat."

Richard looked back at the cave. "You know with all this talk about the treasure being cursed by Captain Kidd. I guess I expected something more than a rockslide. We got away kind of easy."

"Shut your mouth," Marcie said. "Anyway, I think one dead guy makes it a pretty good curse."

Making several rest stops along the way, they slowly made the trip back to the cove. Marcie's injured arm had started to hurt, a deep ache in the bone. But she saw no point in complaining. Soon enough they'd be back in Portland, and she could receive medical attention. Finally, they reached the stretch of beach where Captain Adams had landed. They looked out toward the boat off shore, and saw him wave. In a few minutes, the dinghy had run up onto the sand.

The captain got out of the dingy and eyed the laundry bags. "What do you have there?"

"Rocks," Marcie said. "We're geology students, and we wanted to get some samples from the island."

"Heavy, are they?" he asked.

"They're on the heavy side," she admitted.

He reached down and hefted one. The coins in the bag clinked.

"Pretty heavy. We'll put the bags in the dinghy first, and then I'll take one of you. The other two will have to wait for the return trip. Okay?"

They all agreed.

Richard and the captain got the dinghy into the water, and then loaded the bags on board.

"Who wants to come along?" he asked. "How about the thinnest?"

Amanda stepped forward. She was about to climb into the small boat, when the captain's hand came up. It held a gun.

"Sorry, I changed my mind. No passengers this trip."

"What are you talking about?" Marcie said.

Captain Adams chuckled. "Why, I believe that the three of you have found Captain Kidd's treasure. I've been waiting years for this to happen. To be honest, I'd just about given up hope of ever seeing the day."

"So you're going to leave us here to die?" Amanda said.

He smiled. "You won't die. There'll be another boat along in a couple of days. Now it's true, you'll be kind of cut off until then because there's no cell phone reception out here. But aside from being a little hungry and cold, you should be just fine. And that will give me plenty of time to make my escape to another part of the country. Maybe even another part of the world."

"You'd abandon your boat for a few bags of gold?" asked Marcie.

"It's not my boat, I just lease it. I've got nothing of value to leave behind: no family, no property, nothing I care about. No, me and a few bags of gold will be on the road before the sun sets."

Richard took a step forward, as if he planned to rush the boat.

"Don't be foolish, son, I won't kill you, but a bullet in the leg will be hurting pretty bad by the time the next boat comes."

Richard stopped, his face showing his frustration. Amanda put her arm around him. "It's not worth it."

"Listen to the young lady," Captain Adams said. "You're young. There will always be other treasures."

Having said that, he started to row. Soon he was back on the boat. Giving them a cheerful wave, he started the motor, turned around, and headed back toward Portland.

"Do you think we really will be rescued in a couple of days?" asked Amanda, the anxiety obvious in her voice.

Marcie was about to say something encouraging when the blast came. It was like the entire horizon exploded in a burst of heat and light that shoved them backwards as the boat disappeared in a huge ball of flame.

As soon as she was able to speak again, Marcie said, "I think we'll be rescued a lot sooner than in a couple of days."

Chapter Ten

Two weeks had passed, and Marcie was already anxious to get the cast off her arm. Fortunately, since it was a simple fracture of the forearm, she would be out of the cast in four weeks, but that was two weeks longer than she was happy about. She had been correct about the speed of their rescue. The explosion had been noticed on a nearby island, and a private boat came out to investigate and quickly found them. The Coast Guard also conducted an investigation, as they did whenever there was a boating incident of any magnitude. The state police were also involved because of the death in the cave.

All in all, it had been two weeks in which Amanda, Marcie, and Richard had been up to their necks in red tape. Fortunately, things had turned out all right. No charges were brought against them for trying to find the treasure, which the authorities still seemed to doubt had ever existed. Scott Winston's prints matched those found in Marty's apartment, so that crime was solved. And Maine gun laws were relaxed enough that Richard didn't get in trouble for carrying his handgun on a hike.

Marcie walked down the hall from her office to visit with Amanda. She had been too restless to get much done at work for the last few days, and suspected that she was still decompressing from their adventure. When she knocked on the frame of Amanda's door, she saw that Amanda, too, was staring out the window rather than at her computer screen.

"I'm having trouble focusing," Marcie announced.

"Me, too."

"Yeah, well we came kind of close to being killed. That always takes a while to adjust to."

"Hmm. I have another reason. Richard and I are engaged again."

"Well, congratulations—again. Do you think it will stick this time?"

"I think so. You know I was really impressed at how brave he was when he helped me up from the ground right in front of that guy with a gun. He could have been shot."

"And you were pretty brave as well when you pulled him out of the way of those falling rocks," Marcie said.

Amanda smiled. "I guess there's more to both of us than we thought. I'm figuring that maybe we would make a good couple."

"You've thought that before."

"But after what we've been through recently, I'm pretty much convinced of it."

Marcie smiled. "Well, good luck to both of you."

She turned to leave the office, and then paused. "You know what the Coast Guard said about the cause of the boat's explosion."

Amanda nodded. "There could have been something clogging the fuel lines or faulty wiring."

"Yeah, but they were surprised because that sort of thing doesn't usually happen in a boat that's in frequent use."

"Okay, so what are you getting at?"

"Just think about it. Marty takes a coin from Captain Kidd's treasure, and shortly after he gets knifed to death. Scott Winston tries to steal it back and is crushed under a pile of rocks. Then Captain Adams tries to make off with the treasure, and he ends up being blown to smithereens."

Amanda groaned. "I know where you're going with this— Captain Kidd's curse."

"It will add a lot to the story. And, after all, it is called *The Weird Happenings* column."

"Just hint at it as a possibility. Otherwise we'll be labeled a magazine for crazies."

Marcie grinned. "Don't worry. Everyone loves a good curse."

● ● ● ●

THE END
The Crying Girl
Grave Justice
Ghosts from the Past
When the Last Dance is Over
The Black Dog

ALL THE PREVIOUS MARCIE and Amanda mysteries listed above are available from Amazon in e-book and paperback. You might also check out my website at www.glenebisch.com for a list of all my books currently in print. You can also go through the website to sign up for my newsletter and to contact me. Thanks for reading my book. Reviews on Amazon are always appreciated.

Made in the USA
Middletown, DE
01 October 2021